RED ROOM Diaries
VOLUME I

"Red Room Diaries: Volume I"
is copyright of Ms. Elle X.

Any physical or electronic sharing, redistribution, reproduction, exploitation, electronic transmission, or storage on any other website, in parts or all of the content in any form, is strictly prohibited.

Ms. Elle X

EROTICA AUTHOR — BDSM EDUCATOR

© Ms. Elle X 2020. All rights reserved.

About the Author

Ms. Elle X has been a part of the BDSM Lifestyle for over seven years, as both a 24/7 submissive and professional Dominatrix.

In her professional practice, Ms. Elle has worked with submissive clients along a vast spectrum of ages and sexual fetishes, allowing her to write with a deep level of experience and empathy that a rare few authors possess.

In the summer of 2018, Ms. Elle saw a unique opportunity to expand her Relationship Coaching practice and fuse her kinky experience with her extensive writing background to develop a revolutionary brand of entertainment specifically with couples in mind. That is how LX Erotica was born.

Ms. Elle's evocative short-stories have quickly garnered a reputation as a healthy and erotic alternative to the insecurity and comparison that pornography and traditional erotica often brings, giving couples the freedom to explore and express their deep desires and undiscovered fetishes in a safe and healthy way.

What Readers Are Saying...

"Oh my, I feel like I hit a jackpot when I found Ms. Elle. She captures a true Dominant's feelings and actions like perfectly--I totally feel the emotion. I read her stories to my submissive as her aftercare and she absolutely loves it. Her words are like, well, our life--and that's just beautiful."

   B.E., UNITED STATES

"Jesus Christ I think Ms. Elle might be a genius. Her writing is awesome and just brilliant. Fuckin' bless her."

   J.K., GERMANY

"Ms. Elle's work is just amazing--I'm so in love with it. Just reading her stories sinks me into submission, it's crazy. I can't thank her enough for her writing!"

   A.M., UNITED STATES

"Ms. Elle's stories have granted me with so much enjoyment. I read them at work and they give me such an adrenaline rush that I find myself reading more instead of working! Her storytelling is just gripping and engaging, and I find myself with a dropped jaw and more adrenaline running through me than a quick kinky encounter."

   A.A., UNITED STATES

Contents

About the Author
What Readers Are Saying

1. Owned.. 01
2. Tardy... 10
3. Fire & Ice.. 16
4. Consequences... 23
5. Pin-Up.. 29
6. Cargo.. 36
7. Time to Play... 42
8. Create the Scene.. 43
9. Live the Story.. 44

Social Links

Owned

"Oh I like that little noise. Let's see if you can do it again." I attach the second ____ and kneel before her, gently _____ on the cool ____ as I speak, "You're going to make much more noise than that tonight, slave."

Bruno alerts me of her presence before I even hear the garage door rise upon her arrival. His quick and excited barks continue until she makes her way through the threshold as normal, but the uncharacteristic tone in which she greets the domestic beast serves as my clue that something is not quite right. How she drags herself into the kitchen reinforces my theory, but it is the unmistakable tiredness behind her eyes that offers concrete evidence to my assessment, "Hey sweetie…"

I know this look; I know this tone. This is a kind of exhaustion that begins in the heart and mind; exhaustion so intense that it pushes its way into the body; exhaustion that cannot be escaped or medicated, but a kind of exhaustion that requires a release.
"Hey love," I offer as I approach her with a warm embrace. After dropping her bags on the kitchen counter, she sinks into my chest. I wrap my arms around her in response, gently stroking her back, "Is everything okay?"
Her "no" is muffled as her head remains buried against me.
"What happened?"
She lifts her gaze, and her near lifeless eyes find mine, "Just…" she begins with a sigh, "…just a lot of intense cases today…" She shakes her head, obviously forcing down her emotion, "I know I signed up for it, but I just don't know what the fuck is wrong with people sometimes…"
"What can I do to help?"
Her head falls back against my chest, and after a long, deep breath, her words find their way to me, "Nothing…I just need to be done with this day."
I pull back from her just enough so I can take her face in my hands, "Today is over. You're not doctor anything tonight. You're mine."

"Thank you," she mouths as I kiss her forehead.
"Are you hungry?"
"Starving actually."
"Then why don't you go hop in the shower while I grab some leftovers and wine?"
"Bless you," she replies with a small smirk.
I lean down and slowly wrap her lips up in mine, and when I pull away, I find her eyes closed, as though still lost in my breath. I whisper against her lips, "Go. And return in your black robe."
That is enough to revive a playful spark in her eyes, "Only because you said wine."
I kiss her now smiling lips once more and give her two light pats on the ass as she turns to head upstairs.

"That was wonderful, thank you," she compliments, her voice settling into a peaceful tone, "I needed that."
I watch her head fall back on the side of the couch, exposing her long, graceful neck as she lounges across the seat with her feet on my lap, "You need more than that."
Her smile is slight, "Oh yeah?"
I run my hands under the sheer fabric of her long, black robe, and across her smooth legs, "Oh yeah."
Her eyes remain closed, "And what do I need?"
My tone is nothing but matter-of-fact, "You need to be owned."
Not only do her eyes pop open, but her head snaps up from the armrest unexpectedly quick, "Owned?"
"Yes, as my love slave." I wink playfully to infuse much-needed lightness into the conversation, but she disregards it as her mind is now scrutinizing every detail of my words.
"That's not our dynamic." Her feet have now returned to the floor as she sits up on high alert.
I mimic her body language as I volley back her brusque tone, "It doesn't have to be our daily dynamic to be pleasurable and helpful."
Her brows narrow as the mind I finally calmed is now revved up faster than when she first walked through the door, "So what would that look like?"
I angle my body to face her directly, "It would look like trusting your Master enough to allow Him to release you."
"Master, huh?"

Despite the slight challenge in her voice at this unfamiliar proposal, I maintain the calm confidence she needs, "Yes. To be owned is to have a Master, and that is precisely what you need tonight."
The rise and fall of her chest are obvious, but I am still unsure if the palpitations are being triggered by anxiety or excitement.
"Thoughts?"
Elbows now rest on the tops of her thighs as her hands hold her chin while she stares off into the abyss of thoughts I have inadvertently created, "I honestly don't think 'release' is possible, love—I'm way too in my head…"
I hold out my hand to her, "Challenge accepted."
Her head tilts up to me, and a small spark of excitement ignites behind her eyes as she places her palm in mine as an unspoken agreement.
In this seemingly innocuous gesture, her intrigue serves to fuel to a new level of Dominance, "Wonderful," I begin as I rise from the couch, looking down at her as I stroke her cheek, "The next ten minutes are your own. Then you, and your time, are mine."

Just as my timer is about to notify me of the conclusion to her last ten minutes of freedom, the door of the playroom alerts me to her presence with a gentle "squeak," as she slowly pushes open the heavy timber.
To my immediate displeasure, I find the silken fabric of her robe still covering her form and thus clear my throat to gain her attention, "Do not take another step in my presence until you remove that garment."
Silent surprise fills her eyes as she slides out of the material, allowing it to fall to a pile at her feet.
"Now come, slave."
Her gaze remains locked onto mine as she approaches my chair, and when she reaches the plush fur rug in front of my leather seat, I rise to meet her, "Stand for inspection, slave."

I guide her into the position I desire as I bring her legs wide and place her palms on the back of her head. I slowly circle her, and my words fall on the back of her neck as I twist her hair into a quick braid, "Who owns you, slave?"
Her voice is slight, "You, Sir."
I take a firm grip on her hair and sharpen my voice, "You will address me properly, slave, or you will be punished."
"Yes, Master…"

The marked hesitation in her tone at my new address surges electricity through my veins and directly into my eager cock, "Say it again."
"...Master..."
My left-hand remains in her hair while my right reaches around to her pussy, "That's right, slave. I own you."
Without warning, I push my fingers between her lips to find her body responding quite well to her new position as my vassal, evoking a startled gasp from her uncharacteristically quiet lips. "Who owns this pussy? Who owns this wetness?"
Her hesitant tone is now breathless with the inklings of pleasure, "You do, Master..."
I release my grip from her mane as I abruptly remove my fingers from her, "There's hope for you yet, slave. Now go sit on the V-chair."

We've played on this piece of furniture in the past, yet she shyly sits on a single leg of the "V" with her legs closed, arms crossed, and slightly rounded shoulders, as though trepidatious from inexperience. The contrast of her naked form and reticent demeanor waiting to be unraveled at my command makes my cock jump with excitement, but it is knowing how I plan to make every thought in her racing mind bow to my will that ignites the deep embers of my Dominance.
I keep my sights on her as I approach the rear of the requested chair where I have stowed the necessary implements for tonight's scene, and face the large mirror adorning the entire northern wall, "Is that how you're supposed to sit in this chair?"
"No." Both her expression and tone are oddly ambiguous as she remains still in what I can only assume is a slight test of her Master.
"You will regret testing me again, slave," my voice seethes. "Sit correctly. Now."
She attempts to hide her embarrassed cheeks by deliberately looking down as she slowly readjusts, parting her legs on each split of the "V" as designed, exposing herself in the mirror.
I reach around to her neck to lift her gaze, instructing her to remain still. She silently obeys while I lock the attached posture collar around her neck, forcing her head to remain upright. "I need your head up," I begin as I circle to her front to attach her wrists and ankles to the connected cuffs. "I need you to watch as I break you."
She remains silent aside from a nervous gulp, but her breath noticeably shifts to a steady rhythm of deep, paced breaths as I settle her into the chair. I retrieve from my pocket a set of nipple clamps joined by a deliciously heavy chain, "Now, my slave needs to be properly attired..."

I take her right breast to attach the first clamp, evoking a tiny wince from her panting lips, "Oh I like that little noise. Let's see if you can do it again." I attach the second clamp and kneel before her, gently pulling on the cool chain as I speak, "You're going to make much more noise than that tonight, slave." Her whines intensify as I escalate the tension between the chain and her increasingly aching nipples, "But I am not going to respond to your whimpers, or your moans, or your screams when I break you."

A single tear slides down her cheek at my words, and I gently wipe it away with my thumb as I lower my voice, "I'm not even going to respond to these tears."

She tries to turn her head away, but is prevented by the grip of my hand on her increasingly flushed cheeks, "Tell me your safeword."

"Red," her voice quivers.

"That one word is the only thing I will listen to. Otherwise, you have no say in what happens to you during our time together. Do you understand?"

She nods her head as much as she is able in the confines of the posture collar.

"What was that?" I remove my hand to allow her to answer.

The shakiness in her voice serves to fan the flame of my arousal, "Yes, Master…I understand…"

Chills of pleasure run down my spine as her soft voice and gentle tears yield to my will.

"Better. Now let's see how you're taking to my ownership…"

I slide my right index finger between her legs to find her pussy drenched, "Oh very good, slave." I introduce my middle finger and begin to fuck her quickly, eliciting her first proper moan, "This is how much you like being owned, slave." I push my fingers harder into her g-spot, "This is how much you like being bound and helpless for your Master." I continue to finger her as harsh, ragged breaths escape her lips, "That's right, slave. You have to take it. You're mine."

When her pussy begins to clench around my fingers with pleasure, I pull away from her and push my soaked fingers into her mouth, "Taste my ownership, slave."

She sucks and licks enthusiastically, and when she has adequately cleaned my fingers, I retrieve the anal plug I sneakily set under the chair. I unwrap it from its towel to slide it up to her now soaked slit, spread open for my enjoyment. She jerks slightly at the cool metal against her pussy, so I continue sliding it over her clit and into her juices, warming and prepping it for its final destination. When the large plug is thoroughly soaked, I begin sliding it toward her ass, where I also thoroughly cover with lube, "I own every part of you, slave."

I stop when I reach the location I desire, gradually applying pressure with the tip of the plug. "Including this..." I begin sliding it in but am met with slight resistance from her puckered ass. "Relax for me, girl." In the span of two breaths, she acquiesces, and with a single, forceful push, the oversized plug fills her ass, evoking an aching moan from my slave's lips.
"There we go. Good job, slave." I then retrieve the vibrator I also stowed under her chair, and bring it to her clit. She whimpers as I flip it on; the low, rumbling pressure causing her to writhe within the confines of her restraints. "Struggle all you want, you'll only tire yourself out...and give me a lovely show as you do." I increase the intensity of the vibrator, and her moans quickly compound. "Aching?"
"Mmm-hmm!"
"Excuse me?"
"Yes...Master..." she pants.
I reply by instantly shutting off the vibrator, causing her head to fall against the back of her chair, and a needy moan to escape her lips.

I set the vibrator aside and re-direct my focus to her pinched nipples begging for freedom. In a single movement, I release both the clamp as well as a return of blood flow to her left nipple, causing her to cry out at the sharpness of the sensation. I chuckle at her reaction as I lean down to hover my breath over it, gently kissing and licking the peak of her throbbing flesh.
She whimpers in response, "Oh god please—please—it's so sensitive..."
I ignore her request as well as the needy tone in which it was delivered, and turn my attention to her right breast, causing her stomach to tighten as her body convulses in response to the rush of blood. Her body writhes beneath my feather-soft breath and delicate licks, and she begins to plead with me to bite, suck, pinch...anything to bring my delicious torture to an end.

I continue to disregard her pleas as I abruptly cease and straighten myself to standing, bringing my aching cock to her lips, "Open."
Without hesitation, her parted lips invite me in and she begins to fervently suck around me. My breath catches at the pleasure her skilled lips and tongue provide while I slowly and deeply fuck her mouth. When I am about to come undone, I pull myself from her now drooling mouth and begin stroking myself just inches from her. "You want me to soothe those aching nipples, slave?"
"Oh yes, Master, please!"
My eyes dance with amusement at not just the sight of her, unraveling more and more every moment, but at the growing desperation in her tone for relief.

"Very well," I reply as I quicken my pace around my hard shaft, readying my seed for release across her aching chest. When my warm cum begins running down her chest, my hands begin to knead and pinch her breasts and nipples, releasing cries of pained relief from her dry and panting lips.

When her whimpers begin to quiet, I leave her cum-covered chest and crouch between her legs, "Now let's see how this is doing…" I slowly pull the plug from her until the widest point leaves her, only to slide it right back in at the same, steady pace. Her exhales now begin with the letter "H," as I methodically repeat this process. As I approach the tenth repetition, her back arches from the chair; by the time I double that number, she has sunk into each thrust in syncopation to the rich, heavy beat of the music lightly pounding through the speakers, "Oh you like Master covering you in his cum and owning every part of you, don't you, slave?"
Her eyes remain closed as her body continues to rock to each push but the slight smile is definitive, "Yes, Master…it makes me want to cum…"
"Oh really now?" I reach between her legs with my left hand, "Oh, you're dripping for me, slave. We need to take care of that…"
I push the plug fully into her, where it remains as I grab the vibrator and place it on her clit, "You're going to watch yourself squirt for me, slave."
A series of breathy, choppy "H's" reemerge as I click the vibrator on low.
I rise and lean into her ear, "You're going to watch yourself squeeze out that plug."
Her inarticulate response intensifies as I maintain pressure on her clit.
"You're going to watch yourself cry and scream…and break…"
Her wordless exclamation overpowers the music as I turn the vibrator on high.

I lean away from her so I can look into her needy eyes and stroke her cheek with my free hand, "And when you feel like you can't take anymore…you're going to watch me fuck you."
I lower back down in front of her and begin to lightly pulse the plug without removing it from her as the vibrator continues to engorge her clit.
"Oh…fuck…Daddy!!"
I cease all stimulation and avert all eye contact as I methodically set down the vibrator, rise to stand, place my hands on her forearms, and lean so close to her that the only thing in her frame of vision are my eyes, "Your Daddy isn't here, little girl."
She does everything she can to look away, but I grab her cheeks and hold her gaze, "I am your fucking Master, slave. You exist for my pleasure. Your purpose is to please me. That is your only use."

Her eyes begin to well up with tears as my voice intensifies, "And if you dare disrespect me like that again, you will wear my stripes across your back before I throw you in that cage. Do you understand me?"
The first actual tear falls with the whisper of her words, made practically unintelligible by my grip on her cheeks, "Yes, Master…"
I release my grasp and kneel between her glistening thighs, "Now as I said, I want to see this pussy squirt…" I situate the vibrator once again and flip on the highest setting, instantly causing her to let out a whiney, needy moan.

"Repeat after me…I am your slave."
"I…am…your…slave…" she pants.
"I exist for your pleasure, Master."
"I…exist…oh god…" she begins, "for…your…pleasure, Master…"
I begin to circle the vibrator around her clit, "My purpose is to please you, Master."
"Oh…god…" she pants, "I can't…" Her head flails as much as the fixed posture collar will allow, "My purpose is…" Her moan propels the rest of her statement, "to please you…Master…"
"So are you going to squirt for me like a good little slave?"
Her entire body is igniting with jolts and jerks of pleasure as her enunciations become more sporadic, "Oh god yes Master!"
I fix the vibrator right onto her clit, "Eyes open. I want you to watch."
Her series of "ha" breaths quicken and intermingle with moans, pants, whimpers, and unqualified sounds when I add my fingers to the mix, beckoning her to cum.
Within moments, her pussy tightens in preparation for her orgasm, and I slide out my fingers, "Watch yourself, slave…"

She is half screaming, half crying while I maintain the full stimulation on her clit and watch her juices squirt out of her. "That's a start, but I'm not stopping until you push that plug out as I told you."
Her screaming, crying, moaning articulations only grow in volume as her body shakes and squeezes out the plug.
"Keep going, almost there…"
"I can't!" she bellows, "Its too much!"
I circle her clit with the intense rumbles of the vibrator, my cock now eager and aching to dive into her delicious juices listening to such an intense release of energy pouring out of her.
The moment the plug falls to the floor, I click off the vibrator, and in doing so, I bring the focus to the raw, rabid emotion now flowing from her tired eyes in waves.

I lean into her and cradle her cheeks in my hands, "You're doing so well, sweet girl. That was very well done." My words seem to only fuel the tears, so I lean my chest into her and stroke the back of her head, "Release it all, sweet girl. Release it all." I hold her and continue to stroke her head while warm tears run down my chest until she stills and quiets. I slowly pull away and kneel in front of her to find a soppy, tear-stained face with hazy, half-open eyes. Her head falls slightly to the side of the posture collar as her eyes blink slowly in and out of reality.

I rise to my feet with a satisfied smile and walk to the armoire to retrieve a handful of peanut M&M's, a straw, and a fresh bottle of Gatorade from the cleverly stowed mini-fridge. When I return, her head is cocked against the headrest, her eyes are closed, and her mouth open...all signs of a submissive crashing in subspace. I crouch in front of her and run my hand across her left thigh, "Wake up, sweet girl..."
She seems confused as her eyes slowly blink open and adjust to her surroundings.
I hold up the straw to her dry lips, "Drink."
Within just a few moments, half the bottle is gone, and I pull away to offer an M&M, "Eat."
A hazy smile rises to her lips as she crunches with her eyes still closed.
"There we go...is your energy starting to return?"
Her nod is slight as I pop another chocolate-covered treat into her mouth, her energy building with every bite and gulp until she can once again keep her eyes open and head up.
"How are you feeling?"
Her voice is not just soft, but it radiates a calm and steady peacefulness, "Good, Master. Thank you."
"For what are you thanking me?"
"For breaking me, Master. Thank you. Thank you for giving me what you knew I needed. I wish for nothing more than to serve you."
Her words shoot directly from my heart to my cock, "Then finish your snack so Master may continue."

Tardy

I settle into position on my _____, and by the time he arrives at my side, my heart is pounding with nervous anticipation, but I remain silent and still as he _____ the _____ flesh of my ___ with his strong ____.

According to the time on my car's dash, it is 6:43 pm—thirteen minutes past the time I committed to him, making this my third occurrence of the sort since we instated this protocol mere months ago. So I do what any self-respecting submissive would do--I floor it. Then get paranoid, ease up, and check for cops. Then floor it again to get around a dated burgundy Toyota additionally contributing to my current infraction by driving exactly 17MPH under the speed limit.

As I roll into the driveway, my heart practically stops when I see his car already parked in the garage. I check the clock on the dash once more, which reprimands me with a glaring "6:46" readout. With my purse and three large bags in hand, and already shaky from a heady mixture of excitement and nerves, it takes me what seems like ten minutes to open the door and greet my fate. I trot into the kitchen, toss my bags on the counter, and begin my search for him in his usual places...not in the office...not in the living room...not in the game room...not in the bedroom...

My mind lands on a single remaining possibility as I trepidatiously make my way to the basement door.

I slowly push open the heavy timber and find him resting in his leather chair, with a glass of whiskey in one hand and a cigar in the other. His tight black shirt hugs the muscles of his chest and shoulders and contrasts the crisp grey slacks and sleek belt with silver buckle deliciously well. However, Mr. Monochromes fails to even acknowledge my presence as I greet him with a soft and unsure, "Hey..."

I'm thankful for the low and sultry melodies of classic jazz filling the room as his silence replies to me.

"I'm sorry I'm a few minutes late..." I begin as I approach him.

He exhales a puff of his cigar as his left wrist smoothly rises to his eye line,

"Twenty-one minutes to be exact..."
"Because I went around the house looking for you!"
His head snaps to me in his first visual acknowledgment since I entered the room, "You were looking for me for the last twenty-one minutes?"
"Well...no..."
He rises and stands just inches from me, towering over me and overwhelming me with his energy, "What is our protocol every Monday and Friday?"
I speak to the floor as I reply, "I am to be properly cleaned and attired and meet you in here at 6:30."
He pushes my chin up to force my eye contact, "And yet here you are...fully clothed...no collar to be found...and almost thirty minutes late...for the third time since we've established this protocol..."
The way he emphasized "for the third time," sends chills down my spine, "I'm so sorry, Sir...but I'm here now...I got here as quickly as I could..."
He drops my chin as he releases a slight guffaw, "Oh, so now you're ready to respect my timeline?"
My gaze remains focused on my feet, "I'm so sorry, Sir...how can I make it up to you?"
His brusque tone startles me as he sits back in his chair, "Unless you have some way to travel through time, you can't."
My head snaps up to reveal the alarm on my face, "But I want to be a good girl for you, Sir! Please!"
His tone remains just as cold as the glass he sets down after another drink, "Good girls are punctual. You are selfish."
Tears begin to fall as I drop to my knees and lower my forehead to the ground, "I didn't mean to be selfish, Sir, I'm so sorry!"

As I continue to cry with my face to the floor, I smell a fresh puff of cigar smoke waft through the air around me, followed by the familiar clanking of the whiskey stones against the glass before his voice pierces the whirlwind of my emotion, "Then prove it."
"Oh thank you, Sir! Thank you!" I sniffle as I hop to my feet and begin rapidly removing my clothes, tossing them in a pile beside me before dropping back to my knees and crawling toward his feet, kissing his shoes when I arrive, "Thank you for giving me another chance, Sir. Thank you."
"Selfishly choosing to ignore yet another protocol I see..."
I stop offering kisses, but my now nervous lips remain above his shoes as he continues, "What have I told you is the reason for me having you fold your clothes when you remove them?"
My heart drops at the realization of my mindless oversight, "Because folded

clothes show mindfulness and consent..."
"Look at me."
His terse words pierce my nerves as I angle my head to his gaze. His lips are tight, and his gaze cold enough to chill me as he continues, "And despite knowing that, you are now making me out to look like someone who violates your consent."
The tears begin to resurface, "I'm so sorry, Sir...I wasn't thinking--I just wanted to be ready to serve you as quickly as possible...to make it up to you..."
"You think rectifying disobedience with more disobedience would please me?"
My face contorts as a steady stream of tears now run down my cheeks, "No, Sir...I didn't see it like that...I'm so sorry, I wasn't thinking..."
"No, you weren't." He taps out his cigar and finishes off his whiskey before maneuvering around me to his Armoire of Pain & Pleasure.

"Get on the spanking bench," I hear from behind me, quickly inspiring my obedience. I settle into position on my stomach, and by the time he arrives at my side, my heart is pounding with nervous anticipation, but I remain silent and still as he caresses the alert flesh of my ass with his strong palm. When his hand lifts, I prepare myself for the impending swat, but it does not come. Instead, freshly oiled fingers find my ass, evoking a soft gasp at the surprise sensation. His fingers leave me just as abruptly as they arrived, only to be replaced by a familiar sensation. He steadily pushes the oversized anal plug into me, causing me to moan out a long stream of breath as it fills me.

He offers no encouragement or praise, only additional instruction, "Stand up and put these on." When I bashfully stand and turn to face him, he holds out a pair of black vibrating panties, "We need to work on your focus." As I slide on the delicate fabric, I hear the heels of his loafers echo against the dark wood floor until he reaches his chair. He waits for my eyes to return to him before clicking the remote to the lowest setting. I jump slightly at the gentle rumble against my clit as he controls my pleasure from across the room.

He picks up his whiskey glass and shoots the last bit before addressing me, "Come." I quickly move toward him, kneeling at his feet upon arrival, thankful to have my eyes averted from his as I try to ignore the small distraction between my legs. My head jolts to my left, however, when four whiskey stones fall to the floor along with a trickle of the remaining liquor. "Clean this up."
My head pops up to him, "I have nothing to clean it with, Sir..."

"Are you incapable of retrieving the necessary items?" He begins as he preps his cigar for another light.
"No, Sir..."
"Then go. You have sixty seconds." He lights his cigar, takes a puff, picks up the small remote, and turns up the vibration.
"But Sir..."
"Sixty...fifty-nine...fifty-eight..."
Despite both the pressure of the anal plug and soft rumble from the panties, I leap up and dart out of the room and toward the kitchen as fast as my legs will take me. My heart is pounding and my breath shallow when I burst through the playroom door with the cleaning caddy in tow. His voice rises above the smooth jazz melodies as he gestures for me to come to him, "With just two seconds to spare."

My attention returns to the aching quivers across my clit as I kneel at his feet, pull the cleaning rag from the caddy, and begin wiping up his intentional spill. Out of the corner of my eye, I notice him take another puff of his cigar before the intensity of the vibrations between my legs increases once more. I take two long exhales in hopes of helping control the sensation as I continue.
"How are you feeling?" His tone drips with wicked intent.
"I'm starting to ache, Sir."
"Just starting?"
Four quick breaths emerge from my dry lips when he turns up the vibrations once more.
"That should help."
I whimper as I try to focus on my assignment and gather the whiskey stones. After I have thoroughly cleaned the floor, my furrowed brow finds him, "All done, Sir."
"Good girl. Now go get me a refill." He holds out his glass to me, "You have sixty seconds."
I do not hesitate to grab his glass and run out of the room, thankful for the time limit as a distraction from my aching clit.
When I enter his presence once again, I find him tapping ash from his cigar directly over the side table instead of his designer cigar box with built-in ashtray, "You're eight seconds late..."
"I'm so sorry, Sir," I pant as I make the final steps toward him, reaching his glass out to him, "I accidentally spilled a little bit and had to clean it up..."
"Kneel in position three, facing away from me."
"Yes, Sir." My heart pounds hard and heavy as I get into "spanking position," with my forearms on the floor, back arched, and ass lifted. His hand hits so

hard against my ass, that the force of the strike lurches me forward and I moan out a whimper. He does not pause, however, and hits again on the opposite cheek. The last six swats are delivered equally hard and fast until I forget about the vibrations in my panties and focus on the heat radiating from my ass. I hear the rustling of his clothes against the leather as he settles back into his seat before his voice reaches me, "This table needs to be cleaned."
I bite my lip and furrow my brows in attempts to ignore my now throbbing clit as I turn around to face him and crawl to his side table. I grab the rag and surface cleaner and rise onto my knees to execute my task.
"How are you feeling?" He asks with a knowing smile.
"I ache very very much, Sir."
"Good. Now, when you're done with this, get back on the spanking bench."
"Yes, Sir."

Every lift of my leg, every press of my knee, every slow inch toward the spanking bench tortures me with tedious vibrations, now consuming my pulsating pussy. He passes me and offers his hand as I rise to stand upon arriving at my mark. He clicks off the vibrations, but my clit is still throbbing as he slides my panties down and off my legs.

"Climb on," he instructs. As I settle into position, I hear his zipper and nothing more before I feel the tip of his cock. He takes hold of my hips and pushes himself in, and I moan out a series of breaths at the pressure of both the anal plug and his formidable dick, now pressing against my g-spot.
"Ohh fuck," he seethes, as he picks up the pace, ensuring I feel the full tension in my ass with each thrust of his strong shaft.
"Oh, Sir, please!" I pant between thrusts.
He smacks my ass, "Please what?"
"Please make me cum, Sir! Please!"
His voice is ragged and intense as he continues to fuck me, "Good girls get to cum, not selfish little girls."
"Mmm," I whimper, "Please, Sir! Please! I'll do anything to make it up to you!"
He grabs my hair, pulling my head back, "Yes, you will." He accelerates his pace, "You will take my cum without your pleasure, and you will remember to respect my time in the future."
A loud, needy, whiny protest emerges, but he ignores me as he maneuvers my body for the sole purpose of his satisfaction and release.
His weight against my back, along with the steady pace of his breaths soothes me as I rest under him for a moment of recovery. He pulls his head from my back and begins planting kisses down my spine, making me squirm

and giggle under him. Instant relief overwhelms me when he slowly pulls himself out, leaving my ass stretched by the oversized plug.
"You have one more task before I remove the plug."
"Yes, Sir..." I reply without any desire to protest.
His hands leave warm echoes in their wake as they caress my legs before landing at my drenched and still aching, pussy, "You're going to clean the floor," he begins as he deftly circles my clit, "After I make you cum so hard you push out all my seed." His pressure and pace increases, and in a matter of moments, all of the energy he forced me to contain pours out, along with his cum, in a roaring orgasm. As my body sinks into the bench in blissful lassitude, I feel his warm hand softly land on my back, "Come on, baby, you have to finish your assignment."

He guides me off the bench and onto my knees to the right of our mess, "Stay." His first stop is the armoire for a hand towel and bottle of water, before circling to his chair for the cleaning caddy. He sets the tray on the floor to my left and stands over me, "Look at the mess you made..." He takes a couple of swigs of water, cleans himself off, and slides back behind the zipper of his slacks.
"Is that bad, Sir...?" My voice is soft as I spray down the floor with flushed cheeks and begin wiping up the evidence of our encounter.
He kneels to my level and cradles my face in his hand, "Not even a little. I quite like you messy."
I blush and nuzzle into his hand, "Did I make it up to you, Sir?"
"I told you that was impossible."
The concern flares up in my voice as I lift my head from his palm, "But..."
"You were very contrite and obedient tonight, and I love that. But the way to 'make it up,' to me is simply to do what I ask. I will not be so gracious should I have to address this issue with you again, understood?"
I swallow hard as I try to catch my breath, "Yes, Sir. I won't disrespect your time by being late again."
"Good girl. Now get into position three."
A hazy smile rises to my cheeks as I rest my head against the cool floor with my ass on display for him. His soft touch returns to my back, delicately stroking my skin as his touch travels south, "Just lay there and relax, baby."
I bite my lip and exhale through steady breaths while he gently slides out the large plug, "There we go."
He leans over me and brushes my hair from my face, planting a delicate kiss to my forehead, "Now let's go get you cleaned up."

Fire & Ice

When the ____ has _____ across my _____, his _____ fingers don't hesitate to slither between my ____, and I gasp at his touch. "Oh, what a warm, wet girl..."

My knuckles make contact with the heavy timber three times before I sink to my knees and anticipate his reply. Although this is our standard protocol twice a week, I still find myself overwhelmed with nerves every time I wait in naked silence for him to lead me into his domain.
The slight creak of the door makes my heart pound, but it is the fact that in my surrender, I must look upon his feet before I may look upon his face, which deeply stirs me.
"Good evening, my dear."
His smooth voice hovers above me and chills run up my spine as my first words greet him, "Good evening, Sir."
He crouches in nothing but his black linen pants and lifts my chin for an intense kiss. "Follow me," he whispers against my lips before rising and offering his hand as assistance. As he leads me to the large four-poster bed to the left of the door, I cannot help but notice the arrangement waiting for me. A variety of white candles consume a large portion of both side-tables while a white towel drapes over the large wedge in the middle of the bed. As I get closer, I also notice a cuff attached to each four of the bedposts.

"Lay on your back with your ass on the highest point on the wedge."
"Yes, Sir."
As I crawl into position, my eyes take a quick inventory of a few additional items on the side-table: a long, skinny, candle with the wick still in perfect condition, a small knife, a stainless steel travel mug, and an unfamiliar vile of something mysterious.
"What's in the bottle?"
"Have I ever indulged your curiosity?" His tone is just as curt as his reply was quick.
"No, Sir," I begin as I settle onto the wedge, "I'm sorry."
"Thank you. Now, what kind of thought was that?" He secures my left wrist to the first cuff.
"Proactive, Sir."

"We've discussed this; what kind of thoughts are you allowed to have in here?" He begins as he approaches my left ankle.
"Reactive, Sir."
The soft fur closes around my ankle as he tightens the buckle, "Very good." He proceeds to fasten my right limbs in silence, leaving my thoughts to focus on his occasional glances and confident smirks as he completes his task.
"Now wiggle."
My head pops off the bed, "What?"
"Try to wiggle around."
My limbs are extended to the point of a slight stretch, limiting my movements to only small teeters of my shoulders and chest.
"Perfect," he begins as he climbs on top of me, straddling my chest and consuming my frame of view, "Are you ready to be my good, little canvas?" Although he is not pushing his weight down onto me, the heaviness in my chest lightens my voice to a whisper, "Yes, Sir, I want to please you."
His "mmm" is delivered as more of a growl, "Good girl." His kiss thrusts itself into me with a passion so strong that it pushes all the noise from my mind, and I find myself already becoming free within the confines of my restraints.

He pulls away from me and stretches his arm out to grab the small mystery jar on the side-table. "Close your eyes," he instructs before he brings the bottle close enough for me to see. I feel his weight shift as he re-adjusts himself between my legs. His palms slide from my calves and up my thighs, "Oh," he sighs, "I've been looking forward to this all week."
I'm thankful the arch of the wedge serves as a barricade to my blushing cheeks, "I hope I meet your expectations, Sir."
I feel his weight move toward me as his hands slide over my hips, stomach, and breasts, "Your very presence here exceeds my expectations. Thank you for your desire and trust."
I strain my head up to catch a peek of him, "Thank you, Sir."
His smile is warm, "Lay those blushing cheeks down, my dear." He continues as I re-situate myself into a comfortable position, "You asked about the vile..."
His fingers find my pussy, and he applies some sort of gel in steady circles onto my clit. After a few rotations, an unfamiliar feeling introduces itself as a tingling heat, making my clit throb like he's already used me well.
"Oh god, Sir..."
"How does it feel?"
"Hot, Sir...oh god...it aches...oh my god..."
He increases the pace of the circles, exacerbating the pulse between my

thighs. He abruptly stops, and in the span of a breath, the pulsating heat quells into a cool and intense tingle.
"And what about now?" he asks.
I want nothing more than shut my thighs and grind them together for my release, "Oh god, Sir," I whine, "It's cold and tingles now...mmm...please keep going..."
To my surprise, he does continue to stoke the fire and quickly builds it back up into a roaring flame. His slick finger no longer circles but rapidly runs across my clit in vertical lines. A series of needy whines respond to him as I lightly flail within my constraints.
"I love it when you squirm for me..." he encourages before suddenly pulling away from me, and leaving me right on the precipice of orgasm.

He allows me to moan and whine to my heart's content with nothing but an amused smile in response. He then removes himself from the bed and makes his way to the side-table. Time slows as he picks up the long, skinny candle, and brings the wick to the flame of one of the white ones until it is independently lit. He carefully returns to kneeling between my legs, "How does your clit feel now?"
"So hot, Sir...and throbbing...it aches so much."
"This hot?"
Before I have a chance to ask for clarification, I feel a single, sharp bite on my thigh, causing me to cry out at the surprise sensation.
He waits until I quiet before speaking, "This is skin-safe; it's not going to burn you."
I whine, "It stings, Sir..."
He releases another drop of wax onto my leg, "I know." Followed quickly by another, "I want it to sting."
My left leg jerks against the cuff as I inhale sharply through my teeth in response to the bite.
"Oh, you're going to make such a beautiful canvas..."
A nervous moan is my only reply to his dark promise as hot bites continue landing on my left thigh.
"Make as much noise as you need; its music to my ears."
"It stings, Sir!"
The small bites cease.
"Oh, thank you, Sir!"
He gingerly rises from the bed, "For...?"
My breath is still a slight pant, "For stopping."
"I wouldn't thank me just yet." He grabs the travel mug and sets it against my pussy.

I jump at the surprise sensation, "It's so cold!"
He chuckles, "I'm aware of that."
I try to maneuver myself off of the icy metal as he unclamps my left arm and returns to his position between my legs.
"Hold this." He commands.
My head pops up to see him holding out the flickering candle.
I trepidatiously take it and lower my hand against the bed to steady it.
"No. Hold it over your stomach."
I try to calm my nerves and steady the slight shaking in my hand.
"Good girl." He raises my hand, "Now hold it this far above you, with just your index finger and thumb. If any wax drips, I want it on your stomach, not your hand."
"Yes, Sir."
He moves the travel container, and I hear light tinking as he handles it.
"Is that ice?"
"What kind of thought was that?"
"Proactive. I'm sorry, Sir."
"Good girl, thank you. Now, I have something that should help your leg..."

He places an ice cube against the hot flesh of my inner thigh. I jerk in surprise and release a large drop of wax onto my stomach. I shudder at the wax and drop more onto my torso.
His laughter is soft as he pulls the candle from my hand, "How does your stomach feel?"
My breaths are short and shallow, "It stings so much! More than my leg!"
"That's perfectly normal," he begins as he traces the ice cube over the two large drips of wax on my abdomen. "Does this help?"
I close my eyes and smile in relief, "Yes Sir, thank you."
"Good." He says as he makes his way back to my left hand to secure it, "Now let's get back to your legs..."

"Mmm, yes." He growls as he stands at the side-table. "Bring your head up."
When I lift my head, I see him returning to kneel between my thighs, which are covered in drops of red wax. My breath is still tense from the overload of sensation, "Its what you wanted?"
He strokes his cock while he evaluates his work, "Not yet. But we're getting there."
His words hit me like a gong and resonate in shockwaves to my psyche, "Not yet?"
"Correct. Head down."

He grabs the travel decanter at the foot of the bed and returns the ice to my searing flesh, providing relief in one slow, dripping caress at a time. Delicate waves of water tickle my skin as the ice melts under our mutual heat.
When the cube has melted across my thighs, his frosty fingers don't hesitate to slither between my legs, and I gasp at his uncharacteristically cool touch.
"Oh, what a warm, wet girl..." He works my g-spot until my breath begins to shorten. When he pulls his fingers out of me, he quickly applies a second coat of the previous mystery gel to my clit and does not hesitate to resume his tortuous caresses.
"Oh god, Sir; it aches so bad already!"
His tone drips with amusement, "Good." He grabs my hips and pushes himself into my dripping pussy, "Then you're ready for my cum."
His strong hands grip my hips as he rocks me into him, thrusting pleasure into my g-spot and making me ache for release.
"Would you please make me cum too, Sir?"
His pace remains constant, "You'll have to earn it."
"Yes, Sir," I moan. "What do I need to do to earn my pleasure?"
His hands dig into my flesh and in a few minutes of steady thrusts and sharp breaths, he fills me with his seed. I savor the exquisite look of pleasure on his face and release washing over his body as his head falls back to rest.

"Are you okay, Sir."
His eyes remain closed, but a sweet smile greets me, "Yes, my dear. You..." He breathes, "You are very pleasing."
I try to ignore the raging ache between my legs, "I'm so glad, Sir."
A sharp, guttural breath emerges from his lips as he slides himself out of me, "Now, would you still like to earn your pleasure?"
"Oh god, yes please, Sir."
His smile is wickedly delicious as he redirects his attention to the small bottle of fire and ice.
"No! Not more! I already ache so much!"
His chuckle is dark, "Oh poor baby..."
He closes the bottle and begins his apt reapplication process.
"God, Sir...please! Oh god please let me cum!"
He rapidly flicks my clit, "After you earn it, baby."
"Tell me! Tell me how! How do I earn it?!" I beg as I wriggle within my constraints.
His light laugh returns, "You'll get your release after your breasts are covered in my art."
My head pops up, "No, Sir, please...I can't handle that."
He adds two additional fingers to his delicious torture.

"No, you can't finger me too! Please, Sir, please!"
"I can and I am. So would you like to cum now?"
I am an incoherent mess of senseless pleas from his deft touches, "Yes! Please! I'm so close! Please!"
He removes the stimulation from my clit and slows his fingers down to slow strokes deep within my aching pussy, "So you're ready to earn it?"
I whimper, "Sir, please...I can't handle it."
He slides his fingers out of me and moves them to my clit in slow circles, "Well, we won't know if we don't try..."
"Yes, Sir," I whine.
"That's a good girl." He brings his soaked fingers to his lips, slowly savoring my taste as he licks them clean, "Oh, and I'm going to lap you up after you cum."
"What if I can't, Sir? It stung so much on my stomach!"
"Close your eyes."

After I obey, I feel his weight lift from the bed. His voice travels to my upper left, "You have your safeword; if you genuinely cannot handle what I'm about to do to you, I want to hear it." His words make my pussy tighten as my heart rate accelerates, "Yes, Sir." Although my ears are on high alert, he navigates almost silently as he re-ignites the delicate flame and makes his way back to me. He straddles my torso and I can feel his still firm cock rest against me.
"I love feeling your cock, Sir." It jumps in response.
"Shh" he chuckles, "I need you quiet and still." My body stiffens and I try to shallow my breath to reduce all movement in my chest.
"Are you ready?"
"Yes, Sir," I whisper as I try to ignore the unexpected tingling between my legs at the anticipation.

He does not release the first drop instantly. Instead, he lets me writhe in tortuous inaction. When the first bite does land against my left breast, my entire body jumps in response as loud and choppy "Ha's" exit my panting lips.
"How was that?"
"Mmm," I whine, "It stings so much, Sir."
"Oh no...and we haven't even gotten to your nipples yet..."
My head flies off of the bed, "No Sir, please!"
"Shh. Rest your head, baby."
I continue my protest, "Please, Sir, please...I really can't..."
"Head. Down."

I whimper as I obey, fighting back the tears my nerves are rapidly throwing at me. He does not hesitate to continue his creative project, alternating between my breasts with each hot kiss of wax while I perpetually jerk against my cuffs as I cry out in wordless whimpers and aching moans. When he ceases, my mind stills with him, and I can hear the force of my breath for the first time. He places his heavy hand on my abdomen, "Shh, it's okay baby. You're doing so well. Just relax."

When my breath begins to steady, he slides his hand between my legs, "Oh," he chuckles, "Someone's enjoying this more than they've been letting on..." His pressure against my clit is gentle but quick, beckoning the fire to return.
"Oh god Sir, please! I need to cum!"
"Then you're ready to continue." He removes his touch and before I can protest, a hot drop of wax lands on my left nipple. When I cry out in response, I feel his cock jump against me, "Oooh," he seethes, "That's a good girl." He releases another drop near the first spot.
"Ahh! Sir!"
"Just a few more, baby."
My tears fall in a gentle stream by the time my left nipple is fully covered. He wipes my cheek with his thumb, "You did so well, my love."
"Thank you, Sir," I sniffle.
His voice is soft as he continues the tender strokes against my damp cheeks, "You are earning so much pleasure."
He reaches his right hand behind him until he finds my pussy again, applying a strong pressure against my throbbing clit as he circles it, "You will get as many orgasms as you can handle."
I moan in satisfaction at both his touch and his words.
"But we have to finish the task at hand..."

Consequences

I cry out with _____, but he _____ my _____ and resumes his focus on the ____ ____ . As he continues, _____ begin to fall from my _____, "I'm sorry, Daddy! I'm so sorry!"

The tension in his voice matches the strain of the chain leading me by the neck to his chair, "I hope it was worth it, little one." I scan the room for cues, but the only prepared equipment I see as we reach his leather throne is the largest butt plug and vial of oil on the small table to the right of his chair.

When we arrive, he offers only one word, "Down."
I instantly drop to my knees, and he loops the leash around the front left leg of the chair before heading to the door. My blood pulses harder beneath my heated skin as the sound of the lock echoes through the room—the ominous sound of my submission. He walks back to me without any rush, unwraps the leash, and tugs me up toward him without saying a word. When my torso rests against the front of the chair, his statement is simple, "You were completely out of line to disrespect me like that."
Both my gaze and voice fall to the floor, "I'm so sorry, Daddy…I know that now…"
"Look at me." Only when his eyes can once again invade mine, does he continue, "I forgive you, babygirl. But your misconduct still needs to be addressed."
"Yes Daddy, I understand. I trust you to guide me."
I watch his eyes turn from ice to fire, "Very good girl. That's exactly what Daddy wants to hear."
A shy smile blushes my cheeks as I bow my head in reply, and I feel the weight of his gaze upon me as he keeps me there in silent wait.
As my mind begins to still in his presence, his voice penetrates the silence, "Stand and face me. Good girl. Now give me your panties."
The slight wetness on the delicate fabric makes me shy as I hand them to him. He notices instantly, and strokes them as he speaks, "Are you a wet little girl just thinking about Daddy punishing you?"
His words round my shoulders and push my hands sheepishly in front of me while my already flushed cheeks become rosier, and I look around the room

at all kinds of interesting things that need my immediate attention. He clears his throat and my focus returns to him, "If you're not going to answer me, I'll have to see for myself. Turn around." His words send chills down my spine as they hit the back of my neck, "Come closer." I step backward until I feel the cool strip of leather against the back of my legs.
"There we go. Now pull up your dress." Once I do so, he taps between my thighs until I widen them to match the legs of his chair, "Good girl. Now bend over and grab your ankles." When I do, I instantly become aware of how vulnerable I am to his very close and very personal view, but his response soothes my thoughts, "Mmm, I love you being so exposed to me."

I stand motionless and silent, fully open for his enjoyment, with a deep and steady beat radiating throughout my chest. I then feel his warm breath between my legs as his tongue gently caresses my lips, teasing me before slowly running along my slit, fully revealing my arousal. My breath catches at the surprising sensation, and he continues to slowly stroke my drenched sex with his tongue, being careful to avoid direct contact with my now aching clit. When I begin to whine at the ache he has created between my thighs, he pulls away, leaving me slightly breathless. As my voice quiets, I hear gentle movement behind me, but do not dare move from his commanded position. I begin to hear the familiar sound of his hand around his hard shaft, as he pleasures himself at the view of my naked sex on display for him.

After a few minutes of self-induced pleasure, his pace slows and stills before once again hearing the lid on the bottle of oil pop open. Almost immediately following this small but remarkably powerful sound, I feel multiple drops of oil fall onto my ass. The next sensation to introduce itself to me is the light stroking of cool metal across my ass, evoking an involuntary pucker.
"I'd relax that tight little ass if I were you, babygirl…"
After a few deep breaths, I can release the undesired tension.
"Oh, that's a good girl. Now don't move."
He slowly pushes the entire plug inside of me, and I cry out at its size.
"I know it's a lot, but you can take it. Now lay across my lap—we have unfinished business."
I move gingerly as I get into position on his lap, and once I have settled in, his warm palm strokes the tingling flesh of my ass, "Why are you about to be punished?"
My shyness is overwhelming, "I…I…disrespected you at dinner tonight…"
The foreboding strokes continue, "That's right. And these are the consequences of your actions."

He places his foot over the excess chain of the leash, now in a pile on the floor, further securing my location atop his lap. Then the first strike comes, landing so hard against my ass that my legs curl in an unexpected response. He doesn't instruct me to lower them but simply pushes my calves back down before striking my flesh once more. He does not require me to count this time, as is his normal preference. Instead, I notice the rhythm he is creating with each connection his palm makes to my flesh; the visceral beat of my punishment echoing throughout the room. My whimpers gracefully adorned his melody at the outset, but as he continues, my increasingly loud outcries serve as a crescendo to his symphony, while my sharp, erratic breaths syncopate to the deep pounding in my chest, fully rounding out his musical masterpiece.

The unexpected absence of his hot palm allows me a brief moment of relief until his fingers slide between my legs, "Oh baby—feel how wet you are when Daddy spanks you." I feel his cock jump at this discovery and knowing my response is pleasing him allows me to further sink into subspace as he continues fingering me, "Such a little pain slut, aren't you?"
He moves his attention to my clit, making the task of coherently communicating almost impossible, "Yes...Da...Daddy..."
"Well we can't have that, can we?"
He removes his fingers from my pussy, and the next thing I feel is a slow twist of the anal plug before he pulls it out slightly and shoves it back in. I whimper at the sensation, and he repeats the action. Upon my second whimper, he begins to repeat the process, only harder and faster with each repetition. My whimpers quickly turn to pleas as he ensures every part of my ass will remember the consequences of my actions, and I turn my face down so I can bite his leg as he continues.
"Turn your head. Do not stifle your sounds." When my left ear rests on his thigh once again, he continues, "I need to hear what effect a good ass fucking has on you."

I'm not sure if it is his words or the harsh and rapid pace at maneuvering the plug, but the intensity of the moment evokes a loud and breathless cry, "Yellow!"
He instantly slows his pace, "I hear you, babygirl."
My breath slows in relief when he gently slides the plug out of me, "Oh... thank you, Daddy..."
Then I hear the familiar sound of the vial of oil once again, followed by new drops falling onto my aching ass, "You said 'yellow,' not 'red,' baby. I won't go any harder, but we are by no means finished."

His slick fingers rub the oil thoroughly into my ass before the freshly lubed plug slides slowly back inside. I cry out with displeasure, but he ignores my protest and resumes his focus on the anal plug. As he continues, tears begin to fall from my cheeks, "I'm sorry, Daddy! I'm so sorry!" My outburst releases a wave of tears as he finishes his anal punishment, but his voice soothes as his palm returns to the flesh of my ass, "I know baby, thank you. You did so well."
"Thank you, Daddy," I sniffle.
"But we're still not done yet." The moment his words land on my ear, his palm lands once again on my ass, and the tears resume.
"Ten more, baby, and I want you to count them out this time."

With teary eyes and a shaky voice, I obediently count through the pain of each strike. My reward is instant, however, after the tenth blow, as he returns to my clit, "Oh fuck, baby. I didn't think you could get any wetter—you're soaked you little pain slut."
"Please, Daddy, please!" I moan as he deftly strokes my needy clit.
"Please, what, baby?"
"Please make me cum, Daddy! Please!"
"Oh, you think disrespectful little brats get to cum?"
"I'm so sorry Daddy! I told you! Please! Please! I'm so needy!"
His chuckle is uncharacteristically ominous, "Not as needy as I am. I'm nowhere near done with you." When he abruptly stops his teasing, it is only my erratic breath that fills the air as I sink onto his lap in mental and emotional exhaustion.

His voice breaks through the silence as he begins to slowly remove the plug, "Relax for me, baby."
A series of short exhales convey my relief as the pressure leaves me. "There we go. Good girl."
My mind is still foggy as he gently massages oil onto the skin of my very red and very sore ass, "How do you feel, babygirl?"
My heavy, tear-soaked lids blink slowly as I smile in appreciation of his care, "My head is foggy."
"And your ass?"
"Sore, Daddy…"
"What about your pussy?"
"Needy…Daddy…"
"For what?"
Finding myself overwhelmed with shyness by his intense Dominance, I simply bite my lip and stay silent.
He continues his soothing strokes across my well-oiled ass, "Do you need

Daddy to fuck you?"
A bashful giggle is the only addendum to my previously silent reply.
"I see. Stand and raise your arms, baby."
He helps me stand and steadies me against his chest, "This has had enough contact with your body. It's my turn." He lifts my dress over my head and tosses it to the floor beside him. Once I stand bare before him, my arms fall heavily to my sides, and I lean my back against him. He gives me a sweet kiss on the top of my head before taking my hand and leading me to the spanking bench.

I hesitate as we approach it, "But, Daddy…"
He kneels before me, "Your punishment is over, babygirl. Now it's about pleasure. Will you get into position for me?"
His eyes are soft as he gently strokes my mascara-stained cheek, and I am helpless to resist, "Yes Daddy."
I climb onto the bench, rest my forearms and legs on the padded leather platforms, and he immediately begins strapping me in place. Unable to move and on display for him, I focus on the sounds behind me as I hear his clothes fall to the floor. The sound of his belt slipping through the loops of his slacks, followed by his zipper sliding down is enough to shift the pace of my heart into high gear. The gentle steps of unshod feet approach, followed by the familiar sensation of his hand on my ass, "Are you ready for me, baby?"
"Yes, Daddy!"
"Ask me."
"May I have your cock, Daddy?"
He begins stroking my clit, "Oh that doesn't sound needy at all…"
"Oh, Daddy, please…may I have your cock? I'm so wet for you…please!"
"Better," he says before slamming into me, evoking a delicious outcry from me, and a satisfying, "Oh fuck," from him.

His pace is quick, and his grip on my hips is firm and steady as he uses my soaked pussy for his pleasure. I tighten around him in response to his vigorous maneuvering, sending him over the edge and filling me fully with his cum. His hands and head fall onto my back as his panting breaths tickle my tingling skin. He kisses down my spine as he lifts himself from me and pulls out of me. He says nothing, nor acknowledges me, as he walks over to the armoire to retrieve the vibrator, plugging it into the wall nearest the spanking bench, "It's time for you to cum now." He kneels at my rear as my splayed legs reveal his seed already slowly running out of me, and flips on the vibrator, "I want to watch my ownership squirt out of you before I fuck you again." He flips the vibrator to the highest setting and my body quickly begins to quiver in response. I feel his fingers between my thighs, adding to

my pleasure, "Oh my cum is already dripping out of you, baby..." His fingers thrust deeper into me, "Do you feel how wet you are for me, baby?"
"Yes, Sir!" I cry out, overcome with the pending release of my pent up pleasure, "I'm getting so close, Daddy!"
He pushes his fingers harder into me as the vibrator continues to absorb my clit of waves of ecstasy, "Then squirt it out for me, baby. Show me who owns you."
The power of his words once again pushes me over the edge and I begin to tighten around his fingers.
His dark, delicious chuckle sends tingles down my spine, "Oh that's it baby-- it's dripping down my hand."

I am a shaky, sweaty mess when I finally call out my safeword at the overload of pleasure now too intense for me to handle, "Red! Red!"
Without hesitation, the vibrator clicks off and his fingers slowly slide out of me, "I hear you, baby..."
His wet hand lands on my right hip as he rises to stand behind me. His body closes the space between us as he leans down over me to kiss my sweaty cheek and brow as his tender touch caresses my back, "Was that what you needed, little one?"
Tears of fatigued release continue to drip from my tired eyes, "Yes, Daddy, thank you..."
His kisses move down my spine as his touch follows, "Such a good little pain slut..." His words agitate the butterflies that were just now beginning to settle in my stomach as his touch slides between my legs once more, stroking my slick inner thighs, "Watching you squirt out my cum made me so hard, baby..."
"Then use me Daddy...I'm yours."
He needs no further invitation as he begins to lightly stroke my still throbbing clit, "My little one isn't too sore already?"
"No Daddy," I sniffle, "I want to please you...please fill me with your cum again...please..."
He is slow to slide into me this time as his body lands heavy over mine. I feel his energy consume me as he maneuvers himself into me for his pleasure, "Oh, I love you my sweet girl...thank you for being mine."

Pin-Up

He guides my _____ by the first _____ and steadies it as he attaches a second one to its right. Before I have a chance to even think of moving, he clips a third _____ to the left of my trembling _____.

"Are you going to be ready to leave in about ten minutes?" He inquires as he leans on the doorframe in his delicious navy suit.
"Probably not," I laugh.
His chuckle is light as he shakes his head, "I should put you over my knee…"
"Go for it—at least we'd be late because of you and you'll stop bothering me while I'm trying to finish my makeup." I peek at him in the reflection to find his amusement pushing his eyebrows up, making me giggle, "What, you can dish it out but you can't take it?" His left-hand moves up to his mouth and slides down his chin as he continues to stare me down. I cannot help but giggle again from both playfulness and now slight nerves as he stands upright and nods toward my current seat, "Lift your robe and lay face-down across the bench."
My nerves bubble over into my reply, "I thought you didn't want to be late…"
He crosses his arms, "I don't give a shit."
I drop my makeup brush and turn around to face him, "So it's okay for us to be late because of you, but not me?" I raise my brows, tilt my head, and cross my arms for added emphasis. His chin lifts, his arms uncoil, and he walks straight for me, grabbing my neck and pushing me down against the small, plush bench, tightening his grip as he leans into my ear, "You think you're so tough, don't you?" My breaths shallow as the pressure around my neck increases in tandem with the intensity of his threat, "You're gonna regret this defiance, brat."
His strong grip combined with his body pressing down against mine renders me unable to move, but I push out as much air as I can in reply, "I doubt it…" My words seem to spark fire behind his eyes, as he pulls me up by the neck, with his left hand gripping a fistful of my hair for additional support. When I'm back to sitting, he releases his hands and takes a single step to the left of the bench, "Get on the floor."

I coquettishly adjust my now tousled hair, "No thanks."
His deep breath is obvious as he slides off his suit jacket. When his gaze returns to mine, I see the spark has become a full and roaring flame, "I will not tell you again."
"Good. Saves us some time."
His expression is surprisingly stoic as he simply walks directly past me to our bedroom. I hear his dresser drawer slide open, and after a moment of light rustling, the drawer slides shut and he returns to the bathroom with his pocket knife in hand. He leans his back against the counter, sets the knife aside, and begins to unbutton his cuffs and roll up his sleeves, "Where are you hoping this attitude will take you?"
"What attitude, Sir?" I reply sweetly as I bat my eyelashes.
He subdues a flash of a smile as he reaches for his knife, slowly flipping it open and closed as he speaks, "Remove your robe and get on the floor."
"I thought you weren't going to tell me again..." I sass.
He allows a visible and audible chuckle, "You have five seconds to do so."
"Or what?"
He clicks his knife shut, slides it in his pocket, and looks directly into my eyes, "Or you will very much regret it."
I uncross my arms and place my palms on the bench, slightly lurching my body his way, "You and your little knife don't scare me."
The right corner of his mouth rises into a devilish grin as he steps away from the counter and walks straight toward me. He grabs my upper arm and pulls me up to him in a single move, tossing me over his shoulder just as quickly as he got me to my feet.
As he carries me out of the bathroom, I feign disapproval by hitting his back, "Put me down! I do not consent to this use of force!"
His hand falls heavy on my ass, "Quiet, brat! Unless I hear your safeword, you're coming with me."
"But what about our plans with Steve and Julie?"
He laughs, "Oh we'll address that in a moment."

He sets me down the moment we cross the threshold of the playroom, "Give me your robe." Despite the temptation to push back again, I playfully slide off my robe and hand it to him, leaving me in nothing but my lace, thong panties. He takes the robe but offers no praise, "Get on the cross."
"Ooh, my favorite!" I reply over my shoulder as I trot over to the St. Andrew's Cross, eagerly stepping into my position of subby victory.

"You see, you thought it was a threat, possibly an empty one, when I said you would regret your behavior," he begins as he takes the medical tray from behind the door and slides it around to the front of the armoire, "but that's not what it meant." I try to ignore the increasing pounding in my chest as he begins locating his desired items. "It meant that I'm a man of my word…and I will make sure you regret your behavior."

Every piece of equipment rattling against the metal of the tray strikes my nerves, to the point that I begin lowering my arms just as he turns to face my direction, "Get your fucking arms up." My arms jolt back into position at his command, but it is the calm, cool, confidence strewn across his visage that truly makes me nervous. When he reaches me he quickly, and silently, secures my wrists and ankles to the large "X," before grabbing his phone and triggering a rich, heavy beat to play through the speakers located throughout our secret hideaway. He sets his phone on the tray, takes the training-clicker, and slides it onto my middle finger, "You know the drill—clicking this is your safeword."
"Yep—nothing new and exciting..."
His laugh is nothing more than a series of short exhales from his nose as his shaking head dons a wicked grin. He grabs one of the many clothespins, still freshly clamped on their packaging and resting next to the electric vibrator, flogger, bottle of water, and hand-towel, and brings it to my lips, "Stick out your tongue." His voice is calm and concise, and due to his purposeful lack of reply to my latest bout of mouthiness, I find myself anxiously compelled to obey.

When I do, he places a single wooden clothespin on the tip of my tongue, causing me to wince at the mild bite. When he briefly redirects his attention to the tray once again, I slide my tongue back, only to receive a scolding, "No, back out. He guides my tongue by the first clamp and steadies it as he attaches a second clamp to its right. Before I have a chance to even think of moving, he clips a third clothespin to the left of my trembling tongue, now evoking a surprising amount of drool. Other than a silent and satisfied smile, he goes back to the tray without skipping a beat, now addressing the flesh of my underarm, clamping it down just below my armpit. At first, the pinch is mild, but the more clamps he adds in a row toward my elbow, the more intense the pinch becomes.

I can do nothing but absorb the pain and focus on the music as he makes a row of five clothespins across each of my underarms and inner thighs. My tongue, arms, and legs are now throbbing as I watch him with watery eyes take two of the remaining four clips from the tray and bend down in front of me. My stomach drops as he disappears from my frame of vision and I feel the cool blade of his knife running up my thighs, soothing the throbbing heat from the rows of clothespins. His voice drips with deep intensity as he slides the blade over and under the delicate fabric of my panties, "You need to stay very still…" The cool steel dips into the waist of the black lace and flattens across my mound, "This is a very sharp knife, near a very delicate area…"

My brows furrow with nerves as I shamelessly pant, allowing drool to run down my chin. My stomach tightens as I feel the blade slide back up across my mound and over to the thin black strap on my hips. I feel the dull exterior of the back of the blade press against me as he twists the knife to face the small space between us. With a single tug, the left strip of fabric falls to the front and rear, allow the remaining loop to slide to my knee. He takes the blade and slides it across the aching row of flesh on my right thigh, leaving a light line of moisture in its wake, "Oh…" he chuckles, "look who got their juices on my knife." I feel a wave of heat rush to my cheeks and I want nothing more than to cover my embarrassment, but as my arms are currently strewn up at his command, he continues to taunt as he slices away the rest of my wet panties, "Little pain slut is enjoying this a bit too much…"

He closes the knife, places it up on the tray, and pushes his fingers into me. I moan through drooling lips as he harshly and briefly fingers me, but when he abruptly pulls away, my pleasurable distraction leaves with him, only to be replaced by two familiar pinches on my vulva. When my surprised gasp and subsequent aching moans greet him, his only reply is a dark and delicious laugh. Meanwhile, my breaths are now heavy as I whine in response to the waves of pulsating heat flooding my body. His expression is incredibly pleased, and his slacks incredibly tight, as he stands up and retrieves the final pins from the tray. He clamps each one onto my nipple, and at this point, I am becoming hazy with a rush of sensation and pain, but his voice successfully beckons for my attention, "Does your tongue hurt?" I nod gently as I whine out my confirmation, fighting back tears.
"You're going to do something for me, and then I'll remove the clamps from your tongue."

He takes his phone from the tray and casually scrolls as I watch with wide eyes and racing thoughts. When he places the phone to his ear, my mind voraciously searches for the who and why of his current call. The moment I hear his greeting, however, I have no doubt who is on the other end of the

phone.
"Hey dude…no, no, actually, that's why I'm calling…Sam and I won't be able to make it tonight…"
My stomach drops as he begins to approach me.
"No, no, everything's fine…I'm sorry we'll have to miss…" He is now standing directly in front of me with the same glee as an eager child on Christmas morning. "Could you grab Julie for a moment? Great." He moves the phone away from his mouth and whispers to me, "When I give you the phone, say, 'Hi Steve and Julie.'"

If from the pent-up pain or intensity of the command, I am unsure, but tears begin slowly falling as he returns to the phone call, "Yeah I'm here…great…okay, here's Sam…"
My heart is pounding as though he's holding a gun, and not a phone, to my face as I slur out through insatiably drooling lips, "Hai Sseethe annn Thuullee."
He takes back the phone, "Did you catch that?" In just a moment, a laugh bursts through the deep, heavy beat radiating throughout the room, "That would be three clothespins…"

When I receive confirmation that I am, in fact, the highlight of this conversation, the tears exacerbate their flow across my flushed cheeks. He ignores the liquid emotion flowing from my eyes and chuckles as he continues, "Well, she actually has one more thing she needs to say." He angles the phone away from his mouth as he addresses me, "Tell them you're sorry for making us miss their party." The tears flow steadily now as I shake my head in response to the unwanted humiliation, but as I do not click for my safe-gesture, I obey when he places the phone to my ear for the second time, "I thaawwllee thor thathin usth mith tha tharthee…"
He is laughing as he takes the phone, "She says she's sorry for making us miss your party." After a brief moment of silence, an uproarious laugh emerges, "Twenty-seven total," he laughs, "Well hey, I learned from the best. Sounds good. Alright, man. Later."

He slides the phone in his pocket and wipes the tears from my cheeks, "You did very well, little girl." He removes the right clamp from my tongue, "Steve and Julie were very entertained." I wince as he removes the left clamp, "They wanted a video…or at least a photo…"
My words rush out when he removes the final clamp from the tip of my tongue, "No, Daddy…please. Please, I'll be a good girl I swear." The tears are pouring once again down my drool-covered face, "Please…I'm so sorry I

was such a brat...I'm so sorry Daddy...I learned my lesson...I'm so sorry, Daddy..."

He exchanges the wet clamps for the small towel, "Aww, I'm Daddy again, am I?" He wipes my face as he continues, "You break so easy, little girl." He folds the towel to reveal a clean side and moves up to the flow of tears across my cheeks, "But I don't care about these tears. Do you know why?"

My crying accelerates as the humiliation, pain, and emotion, build.

"Because I think this is exactly what you wanted when you were pushing me —you wanted me to push back." He tosses the towel on the tray and strokes my cheeks with his knuckles, "And unfortunately for you, little one...you pushed hard."

He stands to retrieve the water bottle and tilts my head back as he helps me take small drinks, "So we're going to play a little game."

My nerves make it difficult to catch my breath when he returns to me with the flogger in hand, "For every clothespin I get, you get fifteen seconds with the vibrator." Before I dare ask what he means, he proceeds by taking a step back from me and swinging the flogger down against the clothespin on my right nipple. My surprised inhale is just as sharp as the tug on my skin.

"See, I didn't get that one, so you don't get any pleasure. Let's try it again." Now fully understanding the rules to his sadistic game, and knowing there will be about two-dozen rounds, the tears of defeat return as he swings the velvet lashes again, this time hard enough to pull the clamp from my nipple and cast it onto the floor. I cry out as he offers comfort, "There we go. Now something to take your mind off the pain..."

He reaches for the tray and pulls it close, bringing the vibrator directly to my clit, "Fifteen seconds, baby..." When he flips it on low, my body jerks in response, and I am quickly distracted from anything but pleasure flooding my veins. The pleasure ceases all too quickly, however, when he abruptly shuts off the vibrator and sets it back on the tray. He stands inches from me as his hand slides between my legs, "Let's see if you're ready for round two..." Two fingers push into me without any sense of gentleness, making me gasp with delight. "Oh..." he chuckles, "Such a wet little pain slut."

By the time he gets to the last five clothespins on my left leg, I am a broken, screaming, pleading mess of emotion. "Daddy! Please," I beg, "I can't take it anymore!"

He doesn't move, "What can't you take anymore, baby?"

"Everything!" I cry, "The pain...the teasing...everything...it's all too much..." My voice trails off into tears as he approaches. His eyes are soft above stoic lips as his knuckles stroke my cheeks through my tears. His voice is but a whisper as he leans into my ear, "If you really couldn't take it anymore, you'd click." I moan at the sharp wave of pleasure shooting down my spine as his pointed words fall onto my neck. He pulls away slowly, stopping at my panting lips along the way, grabbing my cheeks and penetrating my mouth with his voracious tongue.

I try to lean into him as he steps away, "Oh more, please, Daddy!"
"More whipping and edging? Gladly."
This time, the velvet strands hit harder than any of his previous attempts, ripping two clothespins from my flesh in a single strike. My outcry evolves to shaking tears at the pain, which quickly fades as the vibrator begins to lightly rumble against my throbbing clit, "You get thirty seconds, but you are not allowed to cum."

After this much edging, a few deftly executed licks could get me off, let alone thirty seconds with my favorite vibrator. I focus on my breath, however, as he forces my half-minute of pleasure, and am just barely able to withstand before he flips it off. "I'm impressed. Let's see if you can be a good girl for the rest of our game."

My eyes find the light through slow blinks as his gentle touch lifts my head, "Oh I know you're tired, little girl, we're almost done..." He brings the bottle of water to my dry lips, tilting my head back in assistance, "There we go." When I've drunk half the bottle, he returns it to the tray, and makes his way to my right ankle, unlatching the cuff and massaging up my leg. He does the same on the left, slowly guiding my legs together and encouraging me to move and stretch.

"Thank you, Daddy," my voice is soft with hazy appreciation, "My hips were starting to ache." His smile is light when he steps back and unbuckles his belt. He pulls his shirt out slowly, making a meal out of stripping for me until he stands fully nude and displaying the magnitude of his primal intentions. "Those hips will have to endure a bit longer," he begins, closing the small gap between us and hoisting my legs up onto his waist, "I need this pussy first."

Cargo

He points his left index finger to the floor and I lower myself to the _____ ____ in front of his _____ as he uncrosses his legs, placing one on either side of me. "Pull out my ____ and show me how sorry you are for your behavior."

I lead her into the grassy patch just outside the restaurant, "Hand me your purse."
"Can we go somewhere more private, Sir...?"
I scoff, "Not a fan of public humiliation, huh?"
Her head drops, "I'm so sorry, Sir...I-I wasn't thinking..."
"Hand. Me. Your. Purse."
She does so without protest, despite the high-traffic location of my choosing.
"Remove your jewelry," I continue as patrons pass us on the sidewalk.
Even with head down, her flushed cheeks are noticeable as she attempts to remove her bracelet, earrings, and necklace as subtly as possible. I open her clutch and nod for her to drop them in, to which she obeys.
"Now your shoes."
"Sir...please..." she whispers, nervously looking around at the passersby.
I lean into her ear, "I will not say it again."

When I pull back, her eyes are wide and her cheeks flushed with embarrassment as she slowly steps out of her red-bottoms and hands them to me with head down. I situate all of her belongings as I offer her next instruction, "You will follow behind me to the car. I want your elbows locked and both arms fully extended as you hold on to my rear belt loop with both index fingers. Understand?" If it weren't for the remaining coals in my veins at her obnoxious disrespect at dinner, I would have found the surprise in her eyes adorable and arousing, but now it simply propels me deeper into the intensity of my Domspace as she reaffirms her consent with a simple, "Yes, Sir."
As we journey to the parking garage, I am hit with a wide spectrum of expressions from curious pedestrians passing us, but the arousing satisfaction surging through me comes from the fact that the same sets of eyes are looking upon her, forcing her to taste her own medicine.
I stay silent until we arrive at the rear of the car, "Release."

In a moment, her downtrodden face emerges to my right as I pop open the trunk and place her things inside, "You will sit silently in the back seat with head down and palms up on your thighs, understood?"
"Yes, Sir."

The ten-minute ride back to the house passes slowly as I create my mental map of the evening's remaining events. When we reach the end of the street and the house is in sight, I bring the car to a stop at the sidewalk and instruct her to exit the back seat as I make my way out from behind the steering wheel. Her expression is confused as I lead her to the trunk and pop it open, "In."
The same alarm returns to her otherwise demure expression as her head jolts up, "I'm so sorry, Sir...please...it won't happen again."
"Oh, I'm confident of that." I chuckle, nodding to the trunk, "Get in."
"But Sir..."
"But nothing. I only allowed you the privilege of riding home with me for safety and legality, but the house is in sight and the street is empty, so get in."
"What if," she begins with a slight shake in her voice, "...I call my safeword..."
"I will always honor your safeword, you know that." I close the distance between us in a single step, grabbing her cheeks and pulling her head up to meet my gaze, "But unless I hear it in the next three seconds, you're going in." The shock on her face almost stirs a loud burst of amusement from my otherwise cold exterior as I begin my count, "One...two...three...okay, in you go." I step away from the trunk and watch the rose-hue of her skin ignite as she climbs in.

This new bondage overwhelms me as I bask in the compact darkness, feeling an intense pulse journey from my chest to my extremities. The unknown possibilities of his primal authority stir up delicious anxiety within me as I hear the ignition cease and the garage door close, indicating our arrival home. I bite my lip and try to calm my breathing in anticipation of his impending retrieval. Instead, the darkness remains and the faint sound of the mud-room door closing echoes in my ears, ushering in a rushing wave of thoughts. After holding my breath as long as I can to hear the door re-open, I am met with silence, and scramble to get my phone from my purse. Beyond thankful I still have 77% battery, I rush out a quick, "Sir..." My heart pounds for a solid minute until I see the time change and text him again, "Sir, are

you there?" Another grueling minute of silence passes before I try again, "Sir...are you going to come and get me?"
When the next minute passes, I begin a new text through teary eyes, "I'm so sorry for my horrible disrespect tonight, Sir. I shouldn't have made that joke and I'm so sorry I embarrassed you in front of your colleagues. It will never happen again. I know I deserve to sleep in here tonight, and I am happy to do it for you, Sir. I hope you sleep well and I'll be dreaming of you." The moment I hit, "Send," the dam breaks, the full remorse of my behavior rushes out, and I begin sobbing like a little girl.

After my tears have calmed into gentle sniffles, an unexpected light hits me, and I blink out the outline of his shadow. His touch is soft against my cheek, "Hello, sweet girl."
I lurch toward him, wrapping my arms around his shoulders, "I'm so sorry, Sir! I love you so much and I'm so sorry! I won't do it again I promise!"
He chuckles and strokes my hair as I nuzzle his neck, "You really thought I'd make you sleep in the trunk?"
"Yes," I sniffle, "You were so angry."
"I stopped being angry when you listened to me outside of the restaurant," he replies, lifting me from the trunk and shutting it behind.
I pull back to look at him, "So this was my punishment?"
That dark chuckle returns, "No, sweet girl," he says as the mudroom door closes behind us, "We're going to take care of that right now..."
Trying to ignore the imaginations of my impending punishment, I remain locked tightly around him. I snuggle into him to savor the mouth-watering scent of his neck and plant gentle kisses thereon as he carries me to the playroom. He pushes the cracked door open with his back, and the first sight I notice as he shuts the door behind us is my jewelry, purse, and shoes laid out neatly on the floor in front of his chair.

He continues to carry me in silence, setting me on my feet upon arrival at his seat. "Give me your clothes," he instructs as he slides into his leather throne. It is only when I am kneeling bare under the power of his gaze, does he address the presence of my personal effects, "Give me your lipstick."
I quickly shuffle through my black clutch and hand him the Mac tube. He sets the lid on the small table to his left and twists the lipstick up through the shaft, "Dark. Excellent." His attention turns to me, "Stand with your palms on the back of your head." Despite my many questions, I silently obey and lock myself into position, deliberately widening my legs as I know is his preference in this stance.
"I noticed what you did; good girl."

My cheeks flush at his praise, "Thank you, Sir."
"Now hold still."
He kneels and takes the lipstick to the border of my right rib, drawing a slow circle followed by what feels like two arches. He then makes another straight line with a curve. I tilt my head down to try and catch a peek at his art project, but instead, he catches me, "Eyes forward."

As he continues working his way across my abdomen with the small tube, I realize what he's doing...marking me...labeling me, and I fight the force of his precisely executed authority that is tempting my knees to fall to the floor, "I'm so sorry again, Sir..."
"If it were up to me, you would have been in the trunk the entire ride home after what you pulled tonight...and all cargo must be properly labeled..."
When the final line has been drawn across my stomach, he stands and grabs my cheeks, bringing the tube to my lips for a reapplication. With a pleased smile at his work, he releases my face and sits back in his chair, placing the lid back on my now dull and half-used favorite matte, "Put on your jewelry and shoes." I try my best to hide my quizzical expression as I obey, actively avoiding his very interested eyes. When I stand there in nothing but his chosen jewelry, shoes, and ambiguous artwork, I vacillate between complete avoidance of his gaze, and quick peeks to determine his mood. His expressions speak for him as he leans onto the right armrest and tucks his chin in his hand, half-covering his devilish smirk, "Come here."

In two clicks of my red-bottoms, my shins make contact with his slacks. He points his left index finger to the floor and I lower myself to the plush rug in front of his throne as he uncrosses his legs, placing one on either side of me. "Pull out my cock and show me how sorry you are for your behavior."
His very words make my mouth dry as I pant in anticipation. I slide my hands up his thighs, grazing his erection with my thumbs as I move toward his belt buckle. My heart pounds with each "tink" as I unhook the black leather and unzip his slacks. I kiss his erection through the thin cotton as I deftly spring him from his boxer-briefs and slide him into my mouth. He straightens in his chair and scoots down to allow me more access. My lips roll over his engorged head and down his shaft, increasing suction as I pull back up, my hand stroking firmly behind my mouth.
"You don't seem very remorseful to me..."
His words shoot straight to my pussy and I whine at both my arousal and his reprimand as my grip and pace grow hungrier for his taste. Sharp "s's" slither through tight teeth as I desperately lap and suck.

"Yes, show me you're a sorry little brat."
I slide my mouth off of him and massage his shaft in long strokes, "Yes, Sir," I pant, "It will never hap..."
He grabs a fistful of my hair and pushes me onto his extensive cock, "I've heard enough from your fucking mouth tonight."
My lips and tongue try desperately to keep up with his voracious pace as he fucks my mouth, pushing my gag reflex upon each thrust until my eyes are watering and my tongue savors the taste of his precum. He stills and holds a tight grip of my mane as he pulls my mouth away from him, "Stand up and turn around."

Still panting from his use, I do as instructed. His words send chills down my spine as his warm hands begin to stroke from my ass to my waist, "Bend over and grab your ankles." The moment I am in the position, I feel his legs make contact against the back of my thighs before his hands greet my pussy. He splays me for his delight before he thrusts into my juices. His hands reach around to steady my hips as he rocks into me, losing himself in his well-deserved pleasures. As his pace sinks into a steady rhythm, he slides his right hand to my pussy, "Oh what a slick little clit..." He rapidly strokes but with a light enough pressure to only tease and not allow any release. I whine for more, but his right hand immediately leaves me and two fingers push themselves into my mouth, "No. You do not get to whine. You do not get your way tonight. You need to remember to whom you belong."

His fingers travel back to my right hip, and both hands dig into my flesh as he accelerates the pressure and pace of his throbbing shaft. My breaths are nothing but a series of staccato "ha's" as he fucks all remaining sass, disrespect, and brattiness out of me.
"Tell me who owns you," he rasps.
"You. Sir."
Fingers sink deeper into my hips, "Say it again."
"You own me, Sir."
The moment my words are released into the air, he releases the full force of his seed into me.
He speaks after a couple of steadying breaths, "Stand up, sweet girl." He slowly slides out of me as I slide back up to standing. He massages from my lower back to my shoulders as I rise, "Feeling okay?"
"Yes, Sir." I cannot raise my voice any louder than a whisper at this point, from both fatigue and humility.
"Good. Stand with your palms on the back of your head as before."
As I get into position, I feel his warm cum drip down my inner thigh. As I

fully spread my legs, warm droplets of his seed continue to land beneath me. I feel my cheeks flush with embarrassment, but I keep my chin up and look forward in futile hopes he won't notice upon his return from the Armoire of Pain & Pleasure. I peek through my left periphery as he cleans himself off and tucks his still alert cock behind his slacks once again. When he turns on his heel, my heart sinks as I am presented with the full intentions for his artwork in the form of a polaroid camera. His smile stirs a carnal rumble in the pit of my stomach as he approaches me, surveying the best distance for his optimal shot. He gives no cue before the flash hits my eyes, momentarily blinding me as he fans the photo to life. In four solid steps, he consumes my frame of vision and holds up the photo for my review.

The moment I see myself in the full magnitude of my current state, I break into a ball of tears, but he holds my chin up, "No. Look at it."
Through dripping mascara, I survey what he has effectively reduced me to; my hair looks like I restlessly tossed and turned all night. My Mac matte is smeared everywhere but on my lips, and across my stomach reads, "Owned by Sir," which is evident as his seed runs down my thighs and into a tiny puddle on the floor.
"Whose are you?"
"Your's Sir."
He releases my cheeks and circles me like a wolf closing in on its prey, "Under your pretty clothes..." His fingers trace up and down my naked spine, "Even with your gems and jewels..." He unhooks my necklace and lets it fall to the floor, "And your fancy shoes..." He re-enters my frame of view, "You are still. Fucking. Mine." He holds up the picture in front of my face, "Right?"
The flow of my tears increases, "Yes, Sir. You own me. I am yours completely."
I can no longer resist the temptation and fall to my knees, whimpering upon the force of my landing upon the cool wood. I spread my legs and bring my chest and forehead to the floor between them, flipping my palms up as I settle. The loud thuds within my chest serve as a soothing metronome as I wait in silence for his response.
"Follow me."
My heart strikes heavy in my chest as he leads me to the left side of the bed, revealing a large cardboard box with an open side. The box contains my pet bed, pillow, and blanket, and a single roll of scotch tape rests on the side-table. He gestures for me to stop when he arrives at the box, and I watch as he takes the photo and tapes it to the inside of the box, "Go ahead and make yourself comfortable; you'll be sleeping here tonight."

TIME TO PLAY

Dear Lovely Reader,

The goal of my erotica has always been to provide curious vanillas, navigating newbies, and experienced kinksters with a healthy and safe way to explore their sexual fantasies and expand their relational intimacy.

In the following two sections, you will find a list of all the tools and toys featured in each story as an easy reference (or shopping list)! In addition, I have provided a set of six story-themed questions to inspire some intimate conversations and kinky play of your own!

Wishing you Healthy Love & Hot Sex,

Ms. Elle X

CREATE THE SCENE

(1) STORY ONE: Owned
- *Anal Plug*
- *Ankle/Wrist Cuffs*
- *Nipple Clamps*
- *Posture Collar*
- *Vibrator*
- *V-Chair (Furniture)*

(2) STORY TWO: Tardy
- *Anal Plug*
- *Vibrating Panties*
- *Spanking Bench (Furniture)*

(3) STORY THREE: Fire & Ice
- *Ankle/Wrist Cuffs*
- *Arousal Gel*
- *Liberator Wedge*
- *Skin-Safe Candle*

(4) STORY FOUR: Consequences
- *Anal Plug*
- *Collar & Leash*
- *Vibrator*
- *Spanking Bench (Furniture)*

(5) STORY FIVE: Pin-Up
- *Clothespins (Wooden, 24-count)*
- *Flogger*
- *Pocket Knife*
- *Training Clicker*
- *Vibrator*
- *St. Andrew's Cross (Furniture)*

(6) STORY SIX: Cargo
- *Lipstick, Instant Camera, Pet Bed, Cardboard Box*

LIVE THE STORY

- Are you curious about another style of D/s? If so, what is it and what about this style appeals to you?

- Are there any new protocols you'd like to incorporate into your playtime or dynamic? What would that look like?

- What are two non-sexual locations on your body that you enjoy receiving touch?

- What is a punishment method you've been curious to give or receive?

- Is there an element of positive pain (spanking, flogging, etc.) that interests you? If so, what?

- Are you interested in public play? If so, what is something you'd like to try in public?

SOCIAL LINKS

WEBSITE: msellex.com

PATREON: patreon.com/ellexerotica

YOUTUBE: youtube.com/c/ElleX

INSTAGRAM: instagram.com/ellexerotica

PINTEREST: pinterest.com/ellexerotica

Printed in Great Britain
by Amazon